Absalom

Absalom

The Failure of the Father Revealed
Through the Weakness of the Son

Shaun Saunders

Shaun Saunders
Atlanta, GA

Contents

Foreword

Absalom is a special text, speaking the inner thoughts of so many—fathered and fatherless. It takes the reader on a journey along a father's fatherhood experience, but through his son's lens. As can be expected, though, the son's recollection of his perspective can only begin with his connection to solid memories, thus, leaving a gap between the period that led to his conception and the emergence of the first solid memory to ignite the perspective. As a result, after the son engages on the path of sharing the father's movements, he must honestly confront that which he does not know, revealing an ignorance. The amazing part is how the son's naïve diligence propels him forward, despite the ignorance being presented as a stumbling block. The son's ignorance manifests itself in various forms. At certain moments, ignorance comes in the form of options, hindsight, unforgiveness, or arrogance; while at other times, it is presented as absence, residence, false

identification, or misinformation. It is even represented as the ever-escaping answer to "Why?"

I seek to address the topics of *father* and *fatherhood*
as the opening to *Absalom*. After all, I am a father; how
hard can it be to define two common terms? As I pen
my thoughts, I, myself, have a manifestation of ignorance. I cannot quite put my finger on it, but some-
thing hinders my ability to adequately explain what
I <u>know</u> *father* and *fatherhood* to be. I know how it feels,
but I cannot put it into words. So, I pivot and reach
out to people I feel influence my fatherhood path. It
is quite the collection of individuals: fathers, mothers,
sons, daughters, old, young, various races, fathered,
fatherless, and no fathering experience at all. I ask two
questions:

1. What is your definition of father?

2. What is your definition of fatherhood?

The answers I receive are mind-blowingly hum-
bling and unexpected. The answers to the first question are different syntactically, but similar substan-
tially. However, the answers to the second question
are rich with a variety of healthy, informed, heartfelt
opinions, revealing exactly why I look to this collection

of individuals for guidance when confronted with my ignorance.

I revisit the *Absalom* text with a more informed perspective, for I am not engaging with the characters from my limited view of their shared experience, I enter with the collective thoughts of my village. Now, instead of making short-range connections and leaving those I cannot connect with dangling, I am able to make long-range connections by allowing various components of the characters' experiences to connect with and rest on the experiences of those within my circle. It is an empowering exercise, allowing me to notice that which is not previously observable.

In *Absalom*, the father's failure casts a shadow. The ignorance of his son's weakness hides behind the shadow of the father's failure. That leads me to wonder, where does the son's weakness reside? It also has me wondering if the father's failure stands alone. Either way, one thing is certain: the son's weakness casts its own shadow, and ignorance hides behind it. This ignorance is pinned to a surface, and it can't be seen; therefore, it can't be moved. So, in the son's case, those who seek to assist and fix what is wrong by looking behind the weakness, prescribe incorrect remedies because the ignorance is not seen. They create diagnoses to represent only what is observable, leading to another set of problems, compounding the original problem, ensuring the weakness will never be found. However, caution must be taken because, yes, the ignorance is pinned, but it still has the ability to "usurp" progress. Therefore, it is actively malignant in its apparent inactive, camouflaged state. Now, I wonder with more focus, where does the son's weakness reside, behind the father's failure, alongside the father's failure, or elsewhere? Also, is the weakness in immaturity or maleness? Those are all distractors from the true problem, though -- the ignorance behind it!

Nevertheless, a son's weakness is elusive, and *fatherhood* may be the answer to this. Perhaps, the point is to help manage the son's weakness so it does not get lost in any shadows but stays in the forefront so it can be cultivated into a strength. *Fatherhood,* then, becomes the experience to deter the concealment of the ignorance. Whereas a *father* represents the individual, *fatherhood* encapsulates the collective state of being that *father*, extending the tentacles of experience and birthing the beautiful range of differences.

So, before you read this wonderfully insightful text, get yourself prepared to go on your own parallel journey, alongside the amazing characters!

Steven Littles

Introduction

As the world violently embraces the unlawful pleasures of an infectious disease, subliminally injected into the mind of humanity, an atmosphere God once created for His sons to affirm Himself as a loving and Everlasting Father has now been contaminated by the fraudulent testimony of sons prematurely exposed to the heartache of a plethora of abominable weaknesses, unrepentantly revealed through the failures of their earthly fathers. The silence, negligence, and provocation of a father's authority within our societies' infrastructure have distorted our children's perception, slowly erasing the possibility of ever reconnecting with the oneness they once shared with their Heavenly God and Father. In the absence of an image designed to reflect the eternal presence of an invisible but loving Father, the fruit of rebellion has risen in the heart of a son, longing to hear those words from his father that will affirm his Godly purpose and existence. A father, the primary source of a son's understanding, his sustainer, and the standard by which he measures his suitability and fitness to succeed in the inherited occupation of sonship, is a Godly model used to expose a son to the nature and character of a Heavenly God. Sons look to their fathers for understanding, affirmation, confirmation, clarity, and meaning. A son is willing, at all cost, to comply with his father's instruction, even when he does not agree if he knows his father speaks on his behalf in accordance with the flawlessness of God's Word unfolded in time but spoken in eternity past. Sons usually spend their entire lives aspiring to live up to the echoing sound of a word previously spoken by a father, determined to affirm their worth throughout the duration of their installation into the responsibility of sonship. With that in mind, it is important to remember that the measure of a father's parental guidance can only be confirmed by the admirable or detestable declaration of his son. As the recipient of his fathering, a son will either render a more favorable verdict of "Great Father" or the more damaging verdict of "Dead Beat Dad," a testimony bathed in the son's experience or lack thereof while standing innocently under the umbrella of the defendant's influence.

As the fatherless struggle to convince themselves that their father's absence is not due to their unwarranted existence, the question of why did he do me that way is temporarily bandaged with an answer that encourages society to continually suppress the truth by telling them it is/was because of human nature. This excuse, most commonly used to rationalize for the offended the defender's offense, has caused many to denounce the ideal of a father's masculine posture, determining his presence to be insignificant within the corridors of the traditional family pedigree. David Blankenhorn, in his book, Fatherless America: Confronting Our Most Urgent Social Problems, addresses this notion by saying,

> "As a cultural idea, our inherited understanding of fatherhood is under siege. Men in general and fathers, in general, are increasingly viewed as superfluous to family life: either expandable or as part of the problem. Masculinity itself understood as anything else other than a rejection of what it has traditionally meant to be male is typically treated with suspicion and even hostility in our discourse. Consequently, our society is now manifestly unable to sustain or even find a reason to believe in fatherhood as a distinctive domain of male activity (Introduction, page 2)."

As you can see, the impenetrable walls of a healthy society must be rooted and grounded on the bedrock of the Godly family. This structure in which all the units are built—a father, mother, and their children—was declared by God to be good because it functions in harmony and predictability with His created order. In Genesis chapter two, God introduced Adam to the tree of the knowledge of good and evil to inform Adam about the state of the earth's chaotically dysfunctional atmosphere prior to his existence and its newly revived functional environment created for the purpose of he and his family's preservation. The Godly family, within the sufficiency of all its parts working together as one, is the primary function God placed in the fabric of society as a shield of health and stability. If at any time the core either decides to redefine its purpose or declare its head of the household as a nonessential part of its design, it then becomes unstable, returning to that once chaotically dysfunctional condition that tried to nullify its existence once before. Blankenhorn's statement targets society's effort to redefine the already clearly defined principle of Fatherhood through the eyes of those afflicted with a dysfunction patterned after the tragedy of the absent father's failures. As a result, society, now a carrier of a disease called "Fatherlessness," has placed its dysfunction on the pedestal of normality, expelling the blueprint for the traditional role of a father from the framework of the God-defined family.

Clearly, God has defined, given meaning to, and provided an explanation for the purpose for which things are created and why they exist, specifically the role of the Father, within the framework of the family as an irreplaceably essential asset whose value should never be taken for granted. Unfortunately, due to an overwhelming vicious number of fathers missing in action, voiding the societies in the world of the kind of policing that seeks to protect and serve its communities with Godly love, the fanatical imagination of the unclaimed has granted the lost sons and daughters of this generation the right to purge unlawfully through a false sense of entitlement.

Rising rates of incarceration and criminal activity, an increase in gang membership, the ignorance of the unlearned, a culture of kids sagging with their pants on the ground, a generation of money lovers, acceptance of the radically extreme non-traditional household, the encouraged course of sexual promiscuity with no consideration for sexual purity and host of other un-mentioned lawless deeds have caused the concerned to question and ask where are all the real fatherly heroes? What has caused them to ignore their responsibility for the innocence of the children they help to bring into this world? Yes, laid down with a sexy, had a booty call that went wrong, made love to their always and forever my lady, while doing the do telling her to call on big daddy, but for reasons unknown have yet to be a father to their children who have lost hope of ever rediscovering or drawing a more accurate conclusion about who a father is and what a father is really supposed to be.

With blinded eyes, dimmed by the irresponsibility of a father's neglect, coupled with the posture of a misguided child's overly indulgent self-proclaimed *'The Hell with My Father'* promotional tour, sons are pressured by the ferocious waves of their own insecurities that have imprisoned them in the innocence of their adolescence. Even in the presentation of the son's masculine masculinity, the lack of harmony within himself regarding the inadequacies of his maleness, never addressed due to his father's absence, will always cause him to jeopardize the integrity of his manhood. Now stuck at that place where the initial contact with their unrecognizable foe first occurred during the immaturity of their adolescents, like most men, the appearance of the son's masculine posture is the deceptive measure used to qualify his evolution from the inherited posture of maleness into the accepted responsibility of manhood. This deceptive presumption that misleadingly suggests manhood is the inevitable crowning of maleness as the sole heir to become the man anointed to sit on humanity's throne, without the dedication of pledging and the legal crossing over into its fraternal order, has caused males to recklessly submit themselves over to a delusional idea of automatic entitlement that asserts because I am male, I am a man. Manhood, however, is not an automatic in the natural maturation of maleness biologically inherited, but rather the highest pinnacle of a matured male's postured evolution that causes him to consciously put forth an effort to willingly embrace his God responsibility without compromising the integrity of his natural character, that will leave an undeniable expression of God's tangible existence.

It is, therefore, an imperative necessity for fathers to graduate beyond the maturation of the sperm they released amidst ejaculation and purposefully mature into the responsibility of a man willingly committed to the evolution of his seed when presented to him in the similitude of his biological form. We must understand that every father is a male, but not every father is a man because a man embraces his responsibility to authentically exemplify the character of God in mankind through the validation of his male progeny. Instead of pridefully standing on the ignorant shoulders of some nonexistent unproven conspiracy theory fabricated by unwarranted notions that deny a son the possibility to become the man his father never figured out how to be, real fathers without envy or jealousy happily seek to confirm their success through the evolution of the son of their man.

"A father is a man that expects his son
to be as good a man as he meant to be."
Frank A. Clark

In a world void, filled with the emptiness of death's sting, its life obscured by a cloud of darkness that at times seems to rob humanity's hope from the once predictable possibility of lights energy shining into the beauty of a day's break, the echoing sound of our sons and daughters' tears have once again, as in the days of Noah, flooded the earth with the untamable fury of their blood gushing from the unhealed wounds of daddy's absence. Until fathers and sons move toward repairing and rebuilding those fences that clearly determine the lines of transparency connecting the continuity of two differently timed purposes and their abilities to coexist inside and outside its limits and the illusive freedoms of its fenced boundaries, the ozone layering of this Godly anointed union's protection will continue to grow numb as a result of a massive hole in the two hearts connecting its core. Sons sometimes aspire to validate their worthiness by separating themselves from the deceitfulness of the man their fathers were without ever seeking to find out what factors contributed to his downfall. With an adamant attempt not to be the male like our fathers, we despise rather than embrace the responsibility of the man God naturally created us to be. We often become the epitome of the male we hated and criticize our fathers for being. Underestimating the value of a father's relevance within the continuity of the son's reality, even amidst feeling the never-ending disappointment of his daddy's failures, has caused sons to turn a deaf ear, hoping to dismiss without ever withdrawing from daddy those life secrets needed to know before he dies.

Absalom: The Failure of the Father Revealed Through the Weakness of the Son is a modern-day anecdote exploring, through the father-son relationship of Absalom and David, the impact of a father's unwarranted absences, the proclivities in his son connected to his failures, the underestimated value of his relevance in the life of a child, and the depth of redemption's reach residing in the uncertainty of a failed father's recovery. Narrated through the sonship of the Superhero leader, the details examining the behaviors of the story's main characters, conflict, rising action, climax, falling action, and its resolution will be outlined within the context of the following questions:

- o Daddy, how could you do me that way? The duel of two natures!

- o Side Effects: Why does My Father's Absence continue to expose its head in the reality of my present?

- o No One To Guide Me! How do I rediscover the purpose for why I was created without you, Daddy?

- o The Daddy Daughter Diary: Where were you, and why were you not there?

- o Better late than Never: O' Now You Want to Be My Father; Why?

With the foundation of its contextual framework cautiously formatted, the integral quality of David and Absalom's unresolved family feud will serve as our biblical bedrock, eclectically narrated through the modern-day rationale of the one and only Superhero Lover! In a concerted effort to expose the continuity of a universal theme outlined within this ancient text, the Superhero will translate the intent of its origin into a more practical amalgamation from each of two conflicting perspectives. For Absalom, the Superhero from a son's perspective, will examine the deep depths of unhealed wounds caused by the failures of the fatherly flawed! From a faltering fatherly point of view, the Superhero will expose us to those triggers behind all the leaks in an old building, causing the continued deterioration of its frame due to the neglect of multiple generations, denying the simultaneous existence of sin's influence anchored at the root of its foundational core. In an effort to ensure you, the reader, are provided with the richest textual taste, the ingredients for this real-time narrative will moisten the heart of fathers towards the agonizing cries for relief from the unhealed wounds of a child's pain and will enable sons and daughters to identify how a loving father tactfully applies icing to admonish all the impeccable quality integrated throughout the beauty of his masterfully crafted cake.

So, without further ado, I introduce to every father that initiated the affliction of the afflicted and to the sons and daughters crippled by the infidelity of their father's insurmountable indiscretions, this a modern-day David and Absalom aberration entitled, *Abaslom: The Failure of the Father Revealed Through the Weakness of the Son.*

Chapter One

From My Father's Side:
The Ignorance of a Son's Weakness
Hiding in the Shadow of a Father's Failures

"When the son has done what is just and right, and has been careful to observe all my statutes, he shall surely live. The soul who sins shall die. The son shall not suffer for the iniquity of the father, nor the father suffer for the iniquity of the son. The righteousness of the righteous shall be upon himself, and the wickedness of the wicked shall be upon himself."
Ezekiel 18: 19-20

How can sons objectively measure the contribution of their father's failure without any appreciation for the unhealthy dose of the ignorance hiding behind the shadow of their weakness?

Torn, questioning the origin, the ancestral relevance or insignificance of the blood that somehow manages to connect the "Super" in my "hero" with the ignorance of a maleness that causes me to neglect the responsibility of my manhood, Judge, I move for the grand jury to investigate the legitimacy of the rationale generations of fathers have used as a means to explain the absence of their existence in their God-ordained position of fatherhood? As the acting prosecuting attorney for this case, case file #02251978, The Product of My Father's Fathers' Mistake, I intend to explain beyond a reasonable doubt the repercussions of the fatherly thorn that for years has continued to reveal itself through the mangled flesh of a father's generational pedigree. Before we move on, however, to present the legal parameters upon which the accused will be indicted, I would like to interject on behalf of the victims, the children of the accused, that the grounds of conviction for this case be based on the Biblical standard of the David and Absalom Tragedy. We feel that the details outlined within the complexity of this unresolved father and son tragedy strongly provide insight, from both perspectives, into those multiple triggers that have created a ferociously intense animosity between the two sides represented in this courtroom. So, we ask you kindly to ensure that all the evidence for this trial is measured on nothing more and nothing less than the uncompromising credibility of your Kingdom legislated word.

As the judge motions to confirm the prosecuting attorney's request and to affirm that his word will be the legal grounds used to determine either the innocence or guilt of the accused, he declares to the ignorance of the rambunctious audience of single mothers, deadbeat dads, and fatherless children to be objective because in a fair trial the defendant is innocent until his/her innocence is dismissed by a verdict of guilty. With the trial set to begin, affirmed as the high-profile case of the century due to the abundance of overwhelming egregious evidence introduced during the preliminary hearing, the judge calls each of the two attorneys to the floor to proceed with an electrifying opening argument they presume will persuade the jury to favor their thinking over any possible contradiction. Like the epic excitement surrounding the buildup of the 2017 Warriors and Cavs NBA Finals trilogy, the two sides have thoroughly examined and are consciously aware of both the strengths and weaknesses the opposition intends to exploit and/or expose. As the Superhero, the lead prosecuting attorney, confidently stands, intent on dismantling the defense of the defenseless, he reminds himself to strike with precision, without being condescending, because striking first will not guarantee his side victory. As an avid basketball fan, he remembers the domination of the historic 73-9 Golden

State Warriors in the first few games of the 2016 NBA finals against the Cleveland Cavaliers and how, after taking an unrecoverable 3-1 series lead, they lost, all because of their immaturity on how to respond appropriately at key moments in the process. Refusing to do a Drammond, leaving his team helpless and shifting the momentum, because of his ignorance, in favor of the defense, he instead engages the jurors with an intensely passionate opening statement that intrigues the audience to engage this dialogue with their more gullible rationale.

Ladies and Gentlemen of the jury, I ask you, What is a father? Just what does a Kingdom Father look like? Has the hurricane of our socially changing climate castrated the traditional role of the Kingdom Father, minimizing his contribution towards the family into the frightening realm of irrelevance or insignificance? How has the absence of our fathers contributed to the failures of our children today? Could it be that the weakness of our sons is the inevitable wrath that stems from the anger of fathers choked by the pains of their failures and the failures of their father's father's absent reflection? Before you try to answer any of these questions, think for a minute about the deep depths that you might have to dive just to touch the tip of a surface clothing the curse of generations fueled with the fury of an unethical madness. Better yet, must I remind you that research shows that 71 percent of all high school dropouts, 71 percent of pregnant teenagers, 85 percent of children with behavioral disorders, 90 percent of homeless and runaway children, 63 percent of youth suicides, 85 percent of youth in prison, and 80 percent of rapists with anger problems come from fatherless homes? So, it is for this reason that we find ourselves gathered together here in this space of time to provide evidence that will show beyond a reasonable doubt that the abominable weaknesses expressed through the wounds of fatherless sons are the consequences of their fathers' failures.

As he speaks with an intensely engaging passion, starkly revealing the burdensome load he was unfortunately forced to carry because of his own personal involvement with this topic, the Superhero grabs the hearts of the listening jurors with an unexpected show of entitled emotions thirsting for the fulfillment of his own father's affirmation asking the jury to ponder on the following questions as they deliberate this case:

- What is a Kingdom Father? What does he look like? Where is mine, and why is he not here?

- Has the father's absence and the tragedy of unethical changes in our social climate caused the role of the father to become an obsolete formality within the bedrock of God's intended/initial concept/context of the Kingdom Family?

- And just how has the absence of fathers contributed to the underdevelopment of the sons and daughters, confronted in their presence by the unlawfully released demons of a father's past, demons left unchained and free to cause havoc in the corrupted flesh of their fatherly pedigree?

As the nervousness centered around this case begins to intensify, the jurors ponder within themselves what might be the most logical response that would finally provide the world with the ultimate resolution that would eradicate this global issue from the face of the earth. The Superhero, understanding the human need to be admonished as the problem fixer, quickly re-engages their thinking with an explanation of fatherhood from a son's perspective.

"Ladies and Gentlemen of the jury, I can see that these questions have challenged you perhaps more than you expected. For generation after generation, society has placed a bandaid on this unhealed wound that continues to expose the bloody hearts of our children and our children's children to a deadly infectious disease called fatherlessness. In a book authored by Dr. Myles Munroe entitled *The Fatherhood Principle,* he reports that 92 percent of all the problems in the world are the result of fatherlessness. The absence of a father in no way nullifies the significance or the insignificance of his contribution to his progeny. The Kingdom model of fatherhood is the epitome of the only universally impartial standard by which every father's legacy will be measured. A father is supposed to be a leader, a source of understanding for his children, a sustainer of the product he produces, and a foundation sturdy enough to bear up under the weight of the family pressures resting on top of him. The effects of my father's absence left me alone to fight with a distorted perception of my God's imagination and my self-image. His absence became the justification I used to illegally bask in insanity, clothed in seduction and masked in the allure of a false sense of entitlement. The pain of his negligence caused the unconquered demons from his unresolved past to, unfortunately, land on my shoulders as enemies fighting to excuse me from the purpose of my future. He left me defenseless, open, and susceptible to the ignorance of any and everything, exposing me to the demand of expectation, which at the time,

I was not mature enough to live up to. Without you, I, I, I mean without him, I was forced to conform to sensual influences bent on pleasing my loins without any respect or regard for the satisfaction guaranteed to accompany my God logic.

So now, after years of silence, searching to find out the reason why and when our fathers decided their love would no longer be there for us anymore, we stand here waiting for the fatherly defendant, DON DADA, who, by the way, did not come willingly, but by force, to somehow enlighten us with the emptiness of gullible words promising to cure sons and daughters from a cancer that has afflicted them for generations? Is it, however, that easy? No, an even better question for you, ladies and gentlemen of the jury, is, Are you going to make it that easy for our fatherly defendant, Mr. DON DADA, to get away with provoking his sons to anger and raping the innocence of his daughter, leaving the beauty of his little girl still waiting for him to show up in all the wrong places? Now, I know that times have changed, and I can no longer presume "No" to be the most logical answer to this question, but I do know that even though the world changes its mind every day, God's Word is immutable and the most stable resource we have in our possession to measure our lives by the Kingdom standards we are supposed to live our lives by. Yes, the answer in a Kingdom dominated by light (knowledge and truth) would be, "No!" It would, however, be negligent of me to overlook the dominance and ignorance of the unlearned, the more liberal thinkers who have determined the role of fathers like our fatherly defendant, Mr. DON DADA, to be obsolete in today's world. Therefore, I, along with my prosecuting team, will leave you with no choice but to hold the defendant, DON DADA, accountable for the murder of his son's destiny! We know that this case will, beyond any reasonable doubt, ignite a great awakening in communities across the world, turning the hearts of the fathers back to the sons and the hearts of the sons back to their fathers. So, to you, our fatherly defendant, Mr. DON DADA, as the recipient of your contribution and your sons' capability of determining the success of your fathering, we, the prosecuting team, have come here this day to inform you per the results drawn from the Kingdom Paternity Test THAT YOU ARE NOT A FATHER!"

Like an emcee, possessed with a universally unorthodox lyrical competence to spit some of the most ferociously venomous bars leaving his opponent in a rap battle cipher speechless, the Superhero turns and purposely drops the mic on the floor right at the feet of the defendant, DON DADA! With a long stare, challenging the defense to reconsider the stupidity with which they would choose to rely on to justify the unexplainable matters of this case, he assured them the punch he just threw was a small sample in a combination of punches he was going to throw to knock out Mr. DON DADA and his defense team. As the jurors exhale, consumed by the intensity of the moment, they look at the judge, sitting at the throne with his gavel in his hand, sweating, and loosening his robe because of the thickness of the animosity cloud that just ignited the uncontrollable flames of the fire burning in the hearts of DON DADA's sons years before they arrived in this courtroom. The judge, hesitantly looking at the defense, calls the defense team up to present their opening argument to the listening audience.

The lead attorney for the defense, the Daily Times' most Diabolical defense lawyer, the Accuser of the Brethren, is one of the most craftily cunning attorneys known for swaying jurors to render not guilty verdicts for deadbeat daddy cases with overwhelming evidence that clearly reveals their guilt. With the microphone now in his hand, he begins to lay the framework for the argument he will use as the basis for what he is confident will be easy to defend.

"Well, well, well! What kind of defense can we give to defend our defendant against these valid accusations the prosecution has just presented to you? I mean, ladies and gentlemen of the jury and to all those of you who have come here to witness this trial, I assure you I in no way mean to be condescending, but I think that the prosecution deserves to be applauded for that, that, that exhaustively passionate opening delivery! It was full, heavy, filled with exceptional wordplay and an extremely thematic intensity displayed with the most exquisite theatrical personification. It was one of the most skillfully crafted arguments I have heard in all my years as the Daily Times' most Diabolical defense attorney. It was valid! It possessed within its framework a credibly sound logic based on truth and reason. It was valid, but being valid is not the same as being the truth. So, let us examine methodically and in detail the nature of the prosecution's argument: The failure or the absence of the father is the only thing in time that caused the weakness of the son.

It is necessary for me to remind you of the prosecution's adamant request that the legal grounds of this case be founded on the Biblical prowess of the David and Absalom Tragedy as it is outlined in the B-I-B-L-E, BIBLE! Well then, because the Bible is the measuring stick upon which we have been informed we must use as our credible reference, point let us take a closer look at a very interesting passage of Scripture that I think will ultimately dismantle the prosecution's validly false argument.

Per the Darby Biblical Synopsis of Ezekiel 18, *The question treated is the allegation of Israel that they, according to the principle laid down in Exodus, were suffering for their fathers' sins. The prophet declares that this principle is not that on which God will act with them, that the soul or life of everyone belonged to God, one as another, and that in judgment, He would deal with each for his own sins, not the son for the father's. God would judge the individual according to his own conduct; the wicked nation was judged as such. Neither was it, in fact, judged for the iniquity of the fathers. The present iniquities of the people made the judgment which their fathers had merited suitable to their own actions. But now, with respect to His land of Israel, the principle of government laid down in Exodus 34:7 was set aside, and souls belonging, as they did individually, to Jehovah, would individually bear the judgment of their own sins.*

With that said, now I am not going to read all of it because it is just too much, but Ezekiel 18:1-4 (AMP) says,

> *"The Word of the* Lord *came to me again, saying, "What do you mean by using this proverb concerning the land of Israel, The fathers eat sour grapes [they sin], But the children's teeth are set on edge'?*

*As I live," says the Lord G*ᴏᴅ*, "you are certainly not going to use this proverb [as an excuse] in Israel anymore. Behold (pay close attention), all souls are Mine; the soul of the father as well as the soul of the son is Mine. The soul who sins will die."*

It appears to me, as well as modern-day theologians, that "the children's teeth are set on edge" because of the sins of their fathers, per the gist of the proverb. The text, when read carefully, however, suggests by saying, "As I live, says the Lord GOD, you are certainly not going to use this proverb," that the Israelites were using this wise saying as an excuse to blame their forefathers for their weaknesses instead of acknowledging their own fault and taking personal responsibility for their own demise. And, by the way, this pericope passage of Scripture succeeds that very well-known verse in the Bible most of our fatherly accusers have used for years to pass the blame of their mistakes on to the shoulders of their so-called daddy issues, "the jealous God, visiting the iniquity of the fathers on the children to the third and the fourth generation of those who hate me." I think based on the revelation of the information shared above, I, just like God, would like to suggest to you that perhaps the baseline the son uses to measure the contribution of a father's failure as the primary cause of his weakness is the same baseline that we must demand be used to determine what percentage of accountability should Sons be held to regarding their own self-destruction.

Please hear me and hear me clearly; I am not suggesting that we should denounce fatherlessness as one of the many sources that have contributed to some of the painful realities our sons have unfortunately been forced to face. What I am saying is that instead of sons always pointing the finger of blame at the fathers, sons must take responsibility for the casualties in their lives they have caused and understand that they are where they are because of their own choices, not because of their father's failures. Now I know that this may sound harsh coming from me, so let me present my argument to you from God's perspective. Ezekiel 18:19-20 (NIV) says, and I quote:

"Yet you ask, "Why does the son not share the quilt of the father? Since the son has done what is just and right and has been careful to keep all my decrees, he will surely live. The one who sins is the one who will die. The child will not share the guilt of the parent (Father), nor will the parent (Father) share the guilt of the child. The righteousness of the righteous will

*be credited to them, and the wickedness of the wicked
will be charged against them."*

The Prophet Ezekiel continues in verse 21 with the echo of God's attitude towards the Israelites who have excused their own infidelity towards God on the foundation of a proverb He has determined to be an unreliable source.

"Therefore, you Israelites, I will judge each of <u>YOU</u> according to <u>YOUR</u> own ways, says the Lord. Repent! Turn away from all <u>YOUR</u> offenses; then sin will not be <u>YOUR</u> downfall. Rid <u>YOURSELVES</u> of all the offenses <u>YOU</u> have committed and get a new heart and a new spirit."

Did you hear it? Did you hear the continuing reverberation of God, speaking through the prophet Ezekiel, redirecting the basis of an illogical rationale used as an excuse by the Israelites for centuries to return the cause of their demise back onto the shoulders of the rightful owner, YOU? Yes, You Sons, in the words of Phil Collins, have declared in your deposition for the jury, and I quote, "To Take a Look at Me Now," suggesting that it is against the odds that your father, the only one responsible for that "Empty Space in your heart," would ever take full responsibility for what clearly God has determined him not to be responsible for. So, we, the defense of our fatherly defendant, Mr. DON DADA, will defend his honor with the integrity of God's unadulterated Word to revise the original framework upon which this case is structured. We believe this case must be changed from "The Failure of the Father Revealed Through the Weakness of the Son" to a more appropriate structure, constructed to inform jurors of an oftentimes forgotten context entitled "The Ignorance of a Son's Weakness Hiding in the Shadow of a Father's Failures." It is with respect that we, the defense, ask if our defendant, in your words, "IS NOT A FATHER," then how can you objectively measure the contribution of your father's failure without an appreciation for the ignorance you hide behind to cover up your weakness? This is the question that we submit to you, the jury, which we intend to accompany with an answer that will echo across the world the sound of responsibility back onto the shoulders of its rightful owner, YOU, the SON afflicted with a disease that thrives in the ignorance hiding behind the shadow disguising the instigator of YOUR weakness, YOU!"

Chapter Two

The Product Of My Father's Father's Mistake

Now these are the generations of Perez: Perez fathered Hezron, Hezron fathered Ram, Ram fathered Amminadab, Amminadab fathered Nahshon, Nahshon fathered Salmon, Salmon fathered Boaz, Boaz fathered Obed, Obed fathered Jesse, and Jesse fathered David.

Ruth 4:18-22

Daddy, how could you do me that way?
The dual threat of two natures!

As the unusually cordial trash talk between the two opposing sides becomes more extreme, both downplaying the furious hatred they share by sending subliminal messages through multiple media outlets, some wonder if the expectation around this case, like the 2017 trilogy between the Cleveland Cavaliers and the Golden State Warriors, would even be competitive or worth watching. With the acquisition of the Superhero, the most successful prosecuting attorney in the nation and a fatherless son, companied with the historical accomplishment of a 73-9 case-winning prosecuting team, the defense, even with the dual threat of their Lebron James and Kyrie Ervin like skilled attorneys, just seem to be unable to match up against all the fire power of the prosecution. Even the depth of the prosecution's witnesses on their bench, blessed naturally with a unique ability to maintain their composure even when overwhelmed by the accelerated pace of the case, has caused fans of this tragedy to bet on this case ending in a sweep. With the allure of fiery talking points seeming to be the only driving force keeping viewers engaged with what most commentators assume will be a one-sided debacle, the prosecution, moving with distinction, hoping to make the most of their home court advantage, stands ready to tip off this case with their first witness.

Ladies and Gentleman of the Jury, please welcome to the stand the grandfather of our victimized sons and daughter and the father of Israel's once most honorably beloved King, this our first victim; sorry, I mean witness; the son of Obed and the grandson of the Billy Dee Williams of the Biblical era, Boaz, one of the most influential progenitors of the Davidic progeny. We present to you, the Bethlehem farmer and sheep breeder, the starting point guard for the defense, Misterrrrrrrrrrrrrr Jesse, the supposedly noble descendant of the tribe of Judah!

Upon his procession through a crowd coupled with the majority of fans cheering the prosecution and others Trumping up his ego with absurd accusations of a media conspiracy theory attempting to undermine the intelligence of viewers by dismissing the arrogance of the unfatherly comments he made unknowingly captured on video, Jesse is ushered to the hot seat by a chorus of sons viciously shouting echoing chants of boos. As he stands, facing an audience filled with the victims of his progeny's assaults, the bailiff extends the Holy Bible towards the clutches of Jesse's reach, requesting for him to place his right hand on the good book while asking him that question: Do you swear to tell the truth, the whole truth, and nothing but the truth so help you, God? After he responded authoritatively with "Yes, I will," the Superhero, like a surgeon, proceeds with his examination of the witness, strategically asking a litany of questions that will expose the cause of a curse that continues to afflict the product of the father's father's mistake.

Jesse, it is imperative for me to remind you once again that you might want to carefully consider your responses to the questions I am going to candidly ask you over the course of my interrogation. You are under oath in the highest-ranking court of law within the universe, and the deceitfulness of the jargon you used to excuse you from your fatherly duties out in the world will not be an acceptable line of logic for you in this case. With that said, why don't we begin?

Within the context of Scripture, I, as well as others, have noticed that your lack of consideration for your youngest son, David, reveals your questioning about the legitimacy of his sonship. In 1 Samuel 16, according to the text, when Samuel presented himself to the elders at the gate in Bethlehem, the elders who stood trembling in fear upon his arrival, comes peaceably to anoint a new king from among your sons, all of which he consecrates except for the youngest David. You choose not to acknowledge him as a son until asked by the prophet, "Are all you sons here? Therefore, I strongly urge you to confidently speak to the legitimacy of your contribution when it comes to the paternity of your son David. Let me assure you before you answer this question, I am fully aware of how your ancestors questioned the legitimacy of Ruth's marriage to your grandfather, Boaz. How Torah law specifically forbids an Israelite to marry a Moabite convert since this was the nation that cruelly refused the Jewish people passage through their land or food and drinks to purchase when they wandered in the desert after being freed from Egypt. How some understand Boaz's death, on the night after his marriage to the Moabitess Ruth, to be a sign that their marriage was forbidden by God. How these events, particularly, cause you to doubt the truth about your right to authentically claim your Israelite genes. So, as a result of your insecurities, you decided to step out on your wife, Nitzevet, with her Caananite maid servant in the hope of having a child that would certify you and your progeny as original descendants of Israel. To your surprise, however, your wife somehow conceived a child by what you still presume to this day to be the seed of another man. Jesse, as you will soon find out, there is more to this story than what meets the eye, but for now, please finish this statement; David is my.............. Is David your son?

Stunned, surprised by the prosecution's thoroughly convincing interpretation of his family history, he hesitantly moves like a shocked crook overwhelmed by the Superhero's revelation centered around the explicitness of a detailed failure he assumed nobody else knew about. Unsure of how to respond, he struggles to put together the right words that would clearly justify the ignorance of his logic. After the judge overrules multiple objections by the defense and the witness continues contemplating how he should respond, he speaks with a tone smothered in frustration.

"No, David is not my Son!" Is that what you want to hear? Well, there you have it. The cat is out of the bag. David was conceived through an act of adultery committed not by me but by my lowdown dirty nasty wife, Nitzevet." Now positioned exactly in the posture of defense, the prosecution sketched out the way they intended this case to be scripted, the Superhero quickly moves to present his first piece of evidence that will undoubtedly contradict Jesse's controversial statement. "Jesse, Jesse, Jesse, I must say in response to your previous statement that I disagree with you. Here is why: According to the paternity test, you are without question 99.9 percent the father of King David. Now I know you are confused, warring within yourself to figure out the possibility of how this could be, so it is for that reason that I am going to expose you to some of the unknown facts of your life.

Ladies and gentlemen of the jury, I present my first piece of evidence to you, exhibit A, Her Secret Silent Within Me. Jesse, if you don't mind, please point to the woman who was your wife at the time of David's conception. Please note that Jesse has pointed to Nitzevet, the mother of David and all seven of his other children, to whom he claims to be their biological father. Amazingly enough, the two of you are still married, despite her supposed infidelity. Interesting! It is imperative for me to insert here that nowhere in Scripture is David's mother ever mentioned by name. Now I am quite sure what I am about to say to you is going to push you into a very tight corner that I can assure you are going to try your damnest to fight your way out of. Your attorneys will most likely, like a good old Milli Vanilli song, sing in harmony a flawed acapella rendition of a defensive masterpiece called "Objection," suggesting the impotence of my words is based on theocratic speculation. That, however, is okay because I think the information I am about to share is time sensitive and extremely important to the integrity of this case. So, let me begin!

As I have already said, it is duly noted that you have been bathing for a long time in the uncertainty of all your Israelite ancestry because of your grandfather, Boaz's, act of affection towards your grandmother, the Moabitess, Ruth. Your illogical rationale, in my estimation, seems to be unreasonable because the Torah Law from which you acquired your information about the unlawful conjugal relations that are to never be shared between an Israelite and Moabite convert was mandated for the converted man with a provided exemption for all Moabite women. This act, of course, was put into law by the Israelites to ensure the continuity of the Israelite progenitors. I say that to make clear that your insecurities within yourself have caused you to make decisions in the ignorance of your understanding. As a result of your ignorance, you decided it to be in your best interest to find your own truth absent the sufficiency of your suitable helper, Nitzevet, your wife. Because of this constant cracking away in the foundation of your existence, you were compelled to act out on this notion of having a child whose ancestry would be unchallenged. So, after years of separation from your wife and children, you orchestrated a plan to have a child with your Canaanite maidservant to officially verify your Jewish lineage. So, you slept with her, or so you thought! What you don't know, however, is that the Canaanite maidservant—you know the other woman—who sure as hell was not going to let you play her like a fool, brought her concern for your request to your estranged wife. Your wife, please raise your hand for the purpose of the courts' recognition, and your hoped to be side piece, the Canaanite maidservant, also present here today, decided on the night of your attempted assault and total disregard for your family to switch places to protect the integrity of your legacy. That sounds just like a good woman who, even after your love for her is gone and what used to be right for you now seems wrong, still allows her heart to be committed to the possibility of your return.

Having cried mountains of tears for years, longing for a father's affirmative touch that would ignite within a son those ferocious aspirations that would motivate him to pursue after, with an unyielding intensity, the manifestation of his destiny, David cried out to you with the tears of his Psalms hoping to legitimize himself as your son, amongst a family that considered him to be a bastard. Because you treated him like his mother was a hoe and he a product of a hoe's ways, he tears his Psalm 51 with the echoing sound of your ignorance, vengefully reminding him every day of his bastardly uprising!

"Behold, I was brought forth in iniquity, and in sin, my mother conceived me."

Psalm 51:5 NKJV

David continues to reveal his discomforts as a youthful male weakened by the absence of you, Jesse, his father, while you, his father, were present with him in the home the whole time.

> *"My brother shuns me like a bum off the street; My family treats me like an unwanted guest. I love you (God) more than I can say. Because I'm madly in love with You (God), They blame me for everything they dislike about You. When I poured myself out in prayer and fasting, all it got me was more contempt. When I put on a sad face, they treated me like a clown. Now drunks and gluttons (Those who sit at the gate) make up drinking songs about me."*
>
> Psalm 68:9-12 MSG

I therefore strongly infer, on the basis of the formatted textual evidence you have so arrogantly laid out for us all to see, within the complexity of a self-published narrative you authored, that you have purposefully exempted yourself from the matriculation of David's infectious weakness caused by the egregious failure of an offense you committed during the promiscuity of your independence. With a contemptuous disposition towards one son, David, you have illegally arrested, shackling them all with the handcuffed attitude of your indignation, the other children in your elitist progeny, derived from the hellish abyss of your antagonist, in the shadowing similitude of your resentment for a child you have yet to claim. Just like an active shooter, massacring the innocence of individuals united under the secured umbrella of one common cause, you have ruthlessly terrorized the progeny of your once over indulgently filled quiver, leaving a mutilated trail of walking dead children's bodies behind for another man to clean up. Like Europe's strategic deployment of racist superiority, the unethical justification for their colonization, and dogmatic oppression of a wealthy African continent, you have consequently inspired and licensed a rebellious movement, smothered in the complexity of contagious inferiority that infuses an introverted self-hatred of oneself, as a result of longing for any sign of a good sample of your fatherly reflection needed to stabilize its foundation, to eat the flesh of their surviving children. Now due to the extremity of the global famine, your fatherless indiscretions have been unfairly laid upon the malnourished frame of your abandoned descendants. You have gluttonously feasted on the fruitful anatomy of your legacy by consuming the underdeveloped flesh of your seed to ensure the continuity of your own preservation without the slightest consideration for the health and nourishment of your own dependents."

"Because of the suffering your enemy will inflict on you during the siege, you will eat the fruit of the womb, the flesh of the sons and daughters the Lord your God has given you."

Deuteronomy 28:53 NIV

With the loud obnoxious shout of "Objection" by the defense, adamant about denouncing the prosecution's projected cannibalistically sketchy profile to an audience of gullible jurors that may unfavorably determine their defendant's fate, before the judge has the chance to sustain or overrule his controversial claim, the prosecutor closes his argument with the reading of the following anonymous letter seared on the flaming tongue of all his longing for years to be heard broken-hearted recipients:

"If you asked to see my scars, I wouldn't pull up my sleeves and show you my arms. I would reach down my throat and pull out my heart to show you all the knicks and cuts which have all but healed. I would ask you to count them, my heart in your hands, then maybe you'd realize that there is one for every time I needed you, and you were absent from the world."

N.I.

"There's nothing worse than a man that can be everything to everybody else…..except a father to his own child!"

Anonymous

Order, order in the court! The judge presiding over the case declares in an imperative voice while banging his gavel on his sound block, commanding both the prosecution and the defense to calm the hell down. Yes, he did tell them, in court, to sit and calm the hell down, or else. The commotion due largely in part to the prosecution's poignant accusations convincingly indicting Jesse, David's father, on the charge of negligence and the defense's continuum of objections censured to counter the insufficiency of the circumstantial evidence, which they believe was distastefully presented as an undeniable truth, has choked the courtroom with a contentious hostility that caused multiple riots to break out between supporters on both sides of the aisle. As the undisclosed details of this case begin to unfold and the disharmony between the two sides represented intensifies, the judge once again calls for order in his courtroom and motions for the defense to move towards their cross-examination of the witness. As the hush of sheer silence suffocates the atmosphere with the cold chill of death, the viewing audience attentively tunes in to see just how the defense will counterargue in order to debunk the alleged truth assumed as inevitable in their opponent's continuously evolving pragmatic theory. With an exhaling breath, releasing an aired uncertainty about the probability of persuading a cold marketed audience to side with an enormous amount of irregularities found within the argued posture of a father's rationale, the defense stands, ready to defend what at first glance appears like a strikingly impossible case to defend.

As the judge anxiously awaits the attorney for the defense to clarify with a response his readiness to cross-examine the witness, the accuser of the brethren makes a surprisingly unusual request he intends to use to reset the prosecution's distorted perception of the witnesses' character. "Your honor, I would like to verbally file a motion with the court, requesting for my client, the witnesses' son, to take the stand alongside his father for the purposes of clarifying the details of their father-son story, a story ignorantly misrepresented by the prosecution in a blatant attempt to defraud the character of my client's personality. It is with the greatest urgency, no matter how unusual I know my appeal may be, that I make this request for the jury to truly understand the value of my client David and his father Jesse's interactions with one another throughout the years to disqualify the protagonist image of my client's person the prosecution has presented hoping to deceitfully undermine the credibility of the defense's case."

At the recommendation of this unprecedented request, the judge calls for both counsels to approach his bench for a further discussion about the defense's monumental motion for both its client and his father to testify simultaneously. As time begins to unfold into the oblivion of the jury's confusion, and the oppressive tick and tock of each minute passing by in slow motion as those privileged to reside in the courtroom anxiously await the judge's verdict on the defense's motion, finally, after what seemed like forever, both counsels walk back to their distinguished desks as the judge pounding his gavel declares for everyone present to hear, "The defense's motion has been granted for both father and son to testify simultaneously. For the purposes of clarity regarding the witness testimony of both father and son, each will be granted a space of time to testify independently even though they will take the stand simultaneously. The prosecution will first question the son in a hotly contested interrogation session entitled, THE MAN IN MY MOTHER!"

Chapter Three

The Man in My Mother

"The absence of a father's affirmation awakens the quieted MAN unlawfully bound in the emotional quiver of a widowed mother's betrayal. My Mother's Man, Jesus, is the essential component that allows the WOKE to effectively engage the SLEEPLESS rebellion of an entitled progeny created by the incompetent semen of fathers unwilling to take responsibility for the dysfunction of the seeds that carry their DNA."

The effortless attempts to rationalize measurable degrees of empathy and compassion for the challenging disruptions that unfairly plague the life of a woman, clothed in the garments of wife and motherhood, have inspired her dependents to yearn intensely for the release of her man, dwelling in the anatomy of the limited bounds she has legally been restricted to. The undoable task of feathering the flames of an adolescent resentment from the under-equipped perspective of motherhood is the masking confusion that leaves the incapable to answer for the unfulfilled actions the capable have been unwilling to perform. Within the natural order of God's original design, though He never intended for mothers to be forcibly burdened down with the weighted mantle of duties forfeited by the immaturity of their seed sowers' maleness, He did provide within His plan a ram in a bush as a serviceable alternative necessary for the restoration of breaches caused by a father's failure. God's expectations for the rolling responsibility of mothers do not include fathering the children of the unfaithful or educating a man on how to be a man from a developmental perspective of a manhood they never have and never will experience.

As the prosecution continues, centering its questioning around the son's potential case shifting comment, the lead attorney deceptively applies a versatility of questionnaire techniques to flip the witness testimony to justify the legal grounds of his argument. Throughout the courtroom, the echoing sound of the witnesses' comment, "I looked up to the Man In My Mother," confused the room, but postured everyone present at the time with a ready-to-learn attitude, anticipating what new revelation they might come to discover on the other side of being WOKE. With everyone sitting upright in their seats, focused on the intensity of the discourse that might stir up the emotions of certain individuals in the courtroom, wondering what the witness meant when he said I LOOKED UP TO THE MAN IN MY MOTHER, the prosecution continues with their questioning asking, "Because most of us, if not all of us, are unfamiliar with your recent comment, can you take some time to provide us with some clarity to help us all understand what you mean? Can you provide us with some personal examples from your own experience or from the experiences of others you may know that would provide a more visible illustration of you LOOKING UP TO THE MAN IN YOUR MOTHER in a more practical reality?

As he leans forward to respond to the questions the prosecution has asked, the witness surveys the audience to measure their engagement, only to discover their faces drooling, ready to feast on the meat dangling off the bones of his answer with all eyes laser-focused on him. With his mike hot and the audience eager to hear him echo in words the understanding of his thoughts, he responds with the following discourse entitled, THE MAN IN MY MOTHER.

"I am a son, husband, and father. The foundation, however, upon which each of these offices stands is in the provided privilege of a manhood hidden within the concrete walls of an immaturity called maleness. Manhood is not the fulfilled promise of entitlement to those fortunate enough to inherently occupy the office of maleness but a privilege to males responsible enough to courageously stand strong under the burdensome plight placed on the male man ("2 Love Her No More," pg. 13). I would just like to reiterate the last line of this quote, pinned in the pages of a book entitled, *"2 Love Her No More"* written by one of the most prolific writers of our time, Dr. Shaun Saunders, that manhood is *"A PRIVILEGE TO MALES RESPONSIBLE ENOUGH TO COURAGEOUSLY STAND STRONG UNDER THE BURDENSOME PLIGHT PLACED ON THE MALE MAN."*

According to Dr. Saunders, "Manhood, however, is not an automatic in the natural maturation of a maleness biologically inherited, but rather the highest pinnacle of a matured male's evolution that enables him to consciously put forth an undeniable effort to willingly embrace the responsibility of a designated office, man, without having to compromise the integrity of his character (*2 Love Her No More*, pg. 13). The quotes I've mentioned above echo important phrases about manhood: "A privilege to males responsible enough," "the burdensome plight," "Manhood is not an automatic." "A matured male's evolution," and the most important of all, manhood is a "Responsibility." In other words, manhood is a choice, a decision that every son, brother, husband, father—every male—has been tasked to obtain in order to model for the descendants birthed out of the fulness of man's quiver, the process of evolution from an immature male into the role of God's responsible man.

At the beginning of creation, God first created a man and stuffed him in a shell called maleness which he biologically inherited from the DNA of the earth. It is important to remember that God only spoke to Adam's Man (the pinnacle of what he internally desired him to become) tucked away in the immaturity of a maleness that stimulates emotions that pluralize the singularity of his most blessed option. So, like Adam, God speaks, calls for the man tucked away in the gender-specific anatomy of a maleness biologically inherited to initiate the man's response to his request. The question I think we first need to answer is, "What happens when the ignorance of maleness usurps the privileged authority of responsible manhood, leaving generations numb to God's presence and clueless on how to respond accordingly to the voice of the one that called? If a male chooses not to evolve and walk in the power of his manhood, the office itself cannot be voided as a nonessential from off the receipt of God's creation, but the qualifying expectation of man will be shifted down onto the shoulders of a ram that God hid in the bushes of his design as an available option to uphold the standard until the male MANS-UP in the responsibility of the office to which he was called! For hundreds of years, males have refused to answer God's call that would escort them into the inherited throne of true masculinity, a throne needing to be covered until the man in every male chooses to become WOKE!

The points I have just explained are foundations that must be acknowledged for the validity of my challenging comment, THE MAN IN MY MOTHER, to be thoroughly understood without undermining the value of its meaning. The absence of a father's affirmation awakens the quieted MAN unlawfully bound in the emotional quiver of a widowed mother's betrayal. My Mother's Man, Jesus, is the essential component that allows the WOKE to effectively engage the SLEEPLESS rebellion of an intitled progeny created by the incompetent semen of fathers unwilling to take responsibility for the dysfunction of the seeds that carry their DNA. As a result of this negligence, the greatness of the greater man in my mother proved to be a more influential presence than the physical disguise of a fraudulent man's promise, stirred up a fit of anger fueled by my resentment because of my ignorance regarding the man of my father's whereabouts.

In his absence, I looked to her for an explanation only he could provide for me to understand how to be the man God expected, without him ever awarding me the privilege of modeling a real-time example of what that expectation actually looked like. While processing my pain through the tragedy of my father's abandonment, I demanded my mother, an eyewitness more traumatized by the firsthand accounts of the ruthlessness revealed by his decisions, to answer for him questions he was nowhere around to answer for himself. The uncalculated fits of my rage that knocked on the door of my mother's broken heart daily, indirectly assaulting her innocence with a ferociously aggressive disdain for my father's failure, conjured up in me a false sense of entitlement that allowed me the unlimited liberty to do whatever I chose until my father answered the WHATS of my WHYS! With my mind numb to the possibility of any fatherly resolve, postured in a way to reject any answer, let alone the truth of the one asked with an answer given that I longed for, my hatred for my father caused me to reflect on in my own life, the shame of those same behaviors that fueled my resentment towards him.

Burdened by the ignorance of a heaviness known as unforgiveness, my attempted posture of resentment towards the man I assumed would justify my critique of my father's integrity caused me to mirror in my own life an almost identical reflection of the man I hated and declared I would never become. The unattended underline conditions that bullied my father around convinced me to dismiss the possibility of there being any inkling of goodness left in him that might be worth me searching through his wreckage to savage. As opposed to avoiding the boisterous waves raging on the surface of his sea of sin, I jumped into the shark-infested depths of his inequity without knowing how to navigate myself through the maze of his dysfunction. In no way was I in a pursuit to salvage the leftover goodness in my father that I was convinced did not exist, but rather to unapologetically justify my emotional hatred for the man that denied himself the privilege of fathering me. To my surprise, the intensity with which I moved to expose his shame pushed me to obsess in the dysfunction of misery he caused at the expense of forfeiting the destiny God specifically assigned to me. The success of becoming what God assigned me to be in a story he scripted was hindered by an arrogance determined to disassociate my legacy from the inherited DNA of the man I despised. I soon discovered that my aggressive attempt to not be like my father paved the road for me to become the epitome of the man in my father I hated.

Now confronted with my insecurities experienced in the realms of two-dimensional realities—sonship and manhood—the uncontrolled measure of my immaturity became exposed once I was prematurely pressured to comply with an expectation of manhood, my biological seed sower never modeled for me to emulate. Struggling with the world's demand to be the reflection of an ideal it despised and sought to eradicate as an obtainable possibility from my God-man DNA, I ignorantly conspired with the world's deception to dismiss the needed role of man, father, and son as essential pieces used to stabilize the nuclear family core. My disdain for the male man species, awarded the privilege of sonship and equipped with the jewels necessary to be crowned on the pinnacle of manhood's highest level of achievement, fatherhood, was crippled by the influence of the visionary's intent on feminizing the power of the God designed man in the minds of people stupid enough to buy into the falsehoods of what they were selling. For years I was stuck on stupid until my mother introduced me to a man that embodied the maturity of manhood, sonship, and fatherhood in his oneness existing wholly in each of these dimensional realities without compromising the integrity of His character. The excellence of His name echoed loudly through the immutability and continuity of His character has compelled me to share with you the identity of the man, the son, and the father that challenged me to embrace my purpose despite the failures of my father revealed through my weaknesses as his son.

It was 1989...... when Mom introduced me to her man, who personally revealed the existence of His person to me in three dimensions of reality and provided me with a one for all remedy that inspired me to take authority over the multiple personalities comfortably residing in the rage of my physical, psychological, and emotional dysfunction. Unaware of these dimensions that separated the depths of my brokenness within the space of three interdependent realms which I relied on to represent an expression of my wholeness, the man in my mother modeled for me the unity of equality that is supposed to be shared between the three personalities cohabitating in the space of my identity. I remember, like it was yesterday, the first thing He ever said to me, affirming with His presence the masculinity of manhood, before He ever spoke a word. He spoke with simplicity, echoing through the frustration that fueled the fire of my disbelief in God's existence in man, declaring effortlessly, for me, that He was a REAL Man! With the words that followed, He challenged me, arguing, "If you, as a man, continue to allow the world to emasculate you from the privilege of your masculinity, then you have chosen selfishly to neglect the responsibility of your call to manhood." With these words, He showed me how to disassociate the immaturities of undisciplined masculinity from the integrity of a God-fearing man fully embracing the responsibility of his manhood. I fought against this notion with an undefeated fighter's reluctance to surrender my hatred towards the goodness of man at the expense of jeopardizing within myself the existence of the greater man in me positioned to cover the weaknesses of a maleness suspended in the air by the ignorance of the world's unrealistic demands.

Now curious, I pursued after His wisdom with the utmost curiosity! His wisdom once again inspired me to see people in the capacity God created them to occupy and not to expect those people to be any more or less than what God naturally created and expected for them to be. To my surprise, even with my unashamed skepticism for His presented posture, He raised me up under the shadow of His wings not out of obligation to make up for those years I lost with my father, but out of the desired want to do, inspired by a personal satisfaction to see me ascend to the highest possible dimensions of my internalized evolution. He modeled for me an example of a man's existence, clothed comfortably in the office of a father's love crippling my pride with a consistent display of actions that left me with no words to defend my hatred.

While basking in the presence of true manhood, I successfully mastered the unpredictability of my physical will to comply with God's designated plan for me within the enduring realms of practicality discovered throughout the history of my experience. With an unusual cadence, exemplified through the perfection of His splendor, His walk echoed for me the sound of real manhood, without ever attempting to be what He understood he was created to be naturally. His posture echoed confidence clothed in the toughness of humility and compassion bathed in deep oceans of wisdom that affirmed His security. He resembled the beginning, middle, and end-product of man's creator's expectation. Psychologically, He forced me into a corner surrounded by the issues that caused me to surrender myself to the error of my ways, with an inspired dialogue that immediately connected the momentum of my movement with an intensity of emotions that massaged my thoughts. He challenged me never to wait for the fatherly offender to change the mind of the fatherly offended and not to wait around for others to bring a change, a change only God possessed me with the power to deliver.

He pressured me to reevaluate an emotionalism, coupled with the misery of my victimized mindset, that moved me to violently protest for the illegal castration of the God-man to be removed from the records of his well-documented family plan. With every ounce of my will, tormented daily by the ignorance of my father's neglect that attempted to emasculate the innocence of my maleness at a young age, I still, like Judas, sought after every opportunity to disqualify the perfection of His man image from my convictions. But He never once slipped into the traps I secretly prepared for Him to fall into. He never once compromised the integrity of His character but maintained a constant consistency that confirmed in the eyes of all broken men like me the validity of His integrity. He was the epitome of a real man and the first real man I had ever known. He, He tactfully showed me the unhealed wounds I masked with a false sense of entitlement that encouraged me to perform like a clown in a circus of dysfunctional behaviors until somebody, anybody, could explain to me the truth of my father's why.

Why did you choose not to father me after you walked away from mom? Why did you not claim me as your son? Why did you not model for me the evolution of a maleness committed to the responsibility of manhood? Why did you never reach for me when I needed you? Why did you not protect me from the pain of my failures? Why did you not show me the posture or attitude with which a real Godly man should approach the pressures of real-life issues? Why, why, no, how could you neglect to preserve the legacy of your name for me, your son? Why did you never make me fill like I was enough?

To this day, I still do not know how he would answer these questions that continue to stalk me day and night, even if I were to ask. At this point, I do not think there is any answer he could give that I would actually believe or accept. I have learned, however, that without the answers to these questions, for years, I forfeited the beauty of my life in the space God designated for me to occupy. To this day, the man in me still longs for the truth of my father's answers to my questions which had deceived me into seeking out therapy sessions with bad habits that have continued to award me opportunities to wallow in the uncertainty of tomorrow. My unsuccessful attempt to dismiss the impact of my father's absence on my subconscious created within me a numbness that signed off for me to prostitute the services of my innocence over to multiple pimps, more commonly known as insecurity, self-hatred, wrath, false sense of entitlement, envy, jealousy, promiscuity, disloyalty, greed, and unforgiveness.

It was not until my pimps were confronted by the man in my mother that I made the decision to reclaim the life space that I had naively allowed unworthy tents to illegally occupy. He stepped to all the haters in my life like a real OG, locked and loaded with lethal rounds of ammunition cased in the wisdom of words that caused my enemies to surrender their will over to the authority of His convictions. My association with His name triggered an overwhelming fear in the heartless persuasion of the ruthless thugs that set out to be identified by me as the King of my streets. But once they attempted to step toe to toe with the true and living King, their aspiration to be the king of my streets faded into the deep-seeding doubts of their impossibility. My enemies still today continue to seek after every opportunity to jump me when assuming I am alone in these streets, but the man in my mother has always been a very present help in my times of trouble. He was, He is my father, that illustrated for me the attitude of approach a son should demonstrate towards a father, conveyed through the personal experience of having to trust himself, with himself within the controversial context of a maleness vs. a manhood and a father and son relationship journeys.

The absence of my biological father's reach for his children within the space of his earthly existence, however, continued to reveal the intensity of his disdain for the recipients of his failed contributions, more catastrophically in the aftermath of his death. The over-exaggerated ambiance of a good father, a relationship for which we, his children, longed to have for over 26 years, was distastefully presented in an obituary smothered with a plethora of lies highlighting achievements that he never lived to see himself. The nail in the coffin, however, was his final words to us recorded in the pages of his last will and testament: "To my children, I leave nothing! Not out of a lack of love, but for my own personal reasons that I care not to explain." The End! Yes, the end! Honestly, dad, I would rather you had said nothing than to leave us with those words. After hearing that, I got my gun and honestly felt the temptation to go back to my father's grave and shoot up his casket, just to award all those ignorantly misinformed about his life another opportunity to bury the real side of him, only his children were awarded the chance to experience. The fury that fueled my rage with the regrets of never pressing him hard enough to get the answers I needed to the questions only my now deceased father could have answered initiated my fall back into the protective clutches of an amazing grace secured in the palm of my Heavenly Father's hand. My resentment fueled my anger; my anger justified my rights of entitlement instigated by insecurities that enabled me to dwell pridefully in the foolishness of my pain, and my pain infected the expectation of my emotions with a disease called numbness that emptied out my reservoir of feelings. This emptiness spilled over into the intimate dimensions of my prospective reach for companionship, burdening my relational endeavors negatively with all outsiders. I placed the heaviness of my father's failures upon the virgin shoulders of those sincere in their love towards me, expecting them to make right for me all that my father made wrong in me.

This was an image of the savage beast residing within the mystery of my undiscovered existence that shackled me up in the misery of my unawakened reality. My dormancy stalled my ability to actively engage in a relationship with my own self-discovery and caused me to identify with the rationale of a failing father's perspective to which I, myself, became a victim and an accomplice in the conspiracy of my family tragedy. My mother's man, Jesus, postured me in the conflicting positions of forgiving the man in the father I hated while acknowledging the expressions of his dysfunctional character spreading the pain of his cancerous wounds in the challenges of my existence. Through Jesus, I came to recognize the egregious efforts I gave towards hating my father were the same energy I needed to give in forgiving the man that failed me in order to rediscover myself and confidently walk in the purposes of a life that God always desired for me. He revived me from an existence smothered in the deadly abyss of a self-inflected hell encouraged by its mentor's unforgiveness. He turned me away from the dark side and turned me to the WOKE SIDE! He is a man's man, a real thug, an OG that sacrificed His life to save the man in mine. Ladies and Gentleman, I would like to introduce to you my mother's man, The Son of Man, the Man King, Kingggggggggggggggg Jesussssssssssssssssss!"

Chapter Four

Failure:
Through the Eyes of the Seed Sower

"Only the recipients of a father's contributions can accurately testify to the truth about either the greatness or the tragedy with which he chose to occupy the office of his fatherly responsibility."

Finally, we have arrived at the point in this never-ending saga, consistently recycled again and again throughout the generations of time, when the defendant, in this case, is granted the generosity of the court to either testify on his own behalf or reject the opportunity to logically dismiss all the accusations against him by refusing to take the stand. This is possibly the most crucial moment in the history of the father-son tragedy that intrigues the interest of the fatherless abandoned worldwide to redirect their attention towards the "Seed Sower," the individual most needed to help affirm and confirm the value of their existence throughout the maturation of their rediscovery process. Within the God-sanctioned authority of every father's voice lies the sincerity of God's attitude of approach, the truth of God's good intentions echoing that familiar sound resonating within the walls of every abandoned child's aspiration to rediscover and become what he or she was naturally created to be through the power of self-manifestation. Now, as they wait to hear the testimony of the father, those abandoned by his neglect has always longed to hear, dad, after placing his hand on the Bible, swearing to tell the truth, the whole truth and nothing but the truth so help him God, has surprisingly decided for the first time to openly testify about the reasons for his lack of involvement in the process of nurturing those positive habits of character in the developmental construct of the seeds he's sown.

Due to this unexpected shift, the prosecution is caught off guard, with this being one of the few times in court history where a father on trial for neglect has elected to testify on his own behalf to justify the merits of his fatherly credibility. Finally, the moment has come for the severely wounded prodigies of the failing fathers to hear the answers to the questions they have always needed to hear in order to free themselves from the addictions acquired outside of the guarantees hidden in the safety of a father's protection. Will he finally provide for the weakness of his seeds a logical rationalization of his thinking that will allow this story to climax towards a positive resolution that sets the afflicted on a course for true healing rather than living in the shallow luxury of their complacency? Can he repeal the mistakes instigated by the arrogant ignorance that he willfully elected to participate in, that created a burdensome plight of resentment in the souls of the fatherless because of his illegitimacy?

With crowds of protestors standing outside, ready to violently express their disgust with this father's audacity to think he should be awarded such a gracious platform to promote the lies disguised in his fantasized truth, they moved unified in the experiences of a father's neglect to stand up against an unrealistic hope of reconciliation between the two parties involved, chanting a catchy phrase slogan entitled "Mute My Father's Mic." Initially, more commonly recognized as a small irrelevant group of disenfranchised children, the movement over time has become more notably recognized as the heavily armed vehicle created to escort the Childrens' Lives Matter Movement into the sphere of the international spotlight. With all the necessary pieces now in place for this trial to proceed, the defense begins its long journey down the almost impossible road of convincing the jury to reasonably doubt the guilt of this father's neglect due to inconclusive evidence. With this strategy standing at the highest pinnacle of optimism for their defense, the defense team proceeds with their plan of action, putting their defendant in the hot seat, calculating that a belief in his testimony would serve him better, even at the expense of his public humiliation through cross-examination.

For the record, can you please state your full name? The defense extended this request to the defendant sitting on the stand. "My name is David, son of Jesse and a descendant from the tribe of Benjamin," the defendant responds. Intent on leaving the prosecution speechless, with no questions left for the jury to examine once their defendant has crossed over into what they believe to be the dark side of no return, the lead attorney for the defense continues saying, "David, son of Jesse and descendant from the tribe of Benjamin, for the sake of not wasting time there is only one question I am going to ask you to answer. The floor is all yours, and you can take as much time as you need. I only ask that you answer this question thoroughly so that when you are done, and we pass the mic to the prosecution, you leave them speechless, convincing them of either your innocence, your remorse, or your ignorance to nullify the arguments upon which they are attempting to convict. David, son of Jesse and a descendant from the tribe of Benjamin, do you understand and comply that you can and will adhere to my request? Please respond by saying yes, I will, or no, I will not!" With a thick cloud of uncertainty boiling in the courtroom, intensified by a furious rage simmering from the bleeding wounds of the unhealed, the defendant responds for the first time in the authoritative voice of his fatherly call, saying, "Yes, I will openly and honestly comply with your request!" The lead attorney, beginning with an overview of the questions from the son's testimony, leads up to his question with the following summation from previous testimony.

"Your son, your flesh and blood, in our session before our brief recess, seemed to passionately desire the answer to questions it appears only you can answer. He said, and I quote, *"Why did you choose not to father me after you walked away from mom? Why did you not claim me as your son? Why did you not model for me the evolution of a maleness committed to the responsibility of real manhood? Why did you never reach for me when I needed you? Why did you not protect me from the pain of my failures? Why did you not show me the posture and attitude with which a real Godly man should approach the pressures of real-life issues? Why, why, no, how could you forget to preserve the legacy of your name for me, your son? Why did you never make me fill like I was enough?* Concluding his passionately convincing discourse with, *"And to this day, I still do not know how he would answer these questions that continue to stalk me day and night, even if I were to ask."*

The one and only question I see fit for you to answer openly, honestly, and with the utmost transparency, David, son of Jesse and descendant of the Tribe of Benjamin, is your detailed response, your answer to the question **Why?** Now please, do not hold back because, according to the prosecution and the children they are standing up for, all the problems with our world today hinge largely in part on our absent fathers' refusal to answer this question. So not to put any pressure on you, but please, please, please understand that your privileged role as the father at the foundation of the family core, according to the prosecution, when neglected, instigates the wrath of fatherlessness assumed by many to be the cause for more than ninety-five percent of the problems in the world. Now, remember, you are the first father ever to grant us access to your thinking on a stage of this magnitude. What you say now will either mend and repair the bridges that have been broken down for years or continue to ignite a blazing fire of deadly conflict between you, the seed sower, and the beauty of the seeds you planted but refused to care for to ensure the safety and health of your harvest that you never gathered. With that said, I leave you alone with the dubious task children across the world have been waiting for years to hear. So now, please share with us all openly, honestly, and transparently the answer to your son's challenging question, **Why?**

With the eyes of millions watching, uncertain about the repercussion or what possibility of resolve may come from the defendant's attempted appeal for mercy from an enraged audience, David, son of Jesse and descendant from the Tribe of Benjamin, speaks about the truth of his negligence from the unfamiliar perspective of the fatherly experience, in a monologue entitled, *The Fatherless: From A Father's Perspective!* "Hem, ahem," clearing his throat before addressing a packed courtroom of wounded descendants eagerly anticipating the resolve with which he better speak when moving to justify the reasons for his continued absence in the lives of the neglected, David nervously sits up, posturing himself like a bully about to get jumped by a crowd of individuals seeking revenge, as he prepares himself to address the victims of his contributions.

"I, I am here today in this very intense setting, fueled by the uncontrollable flames of a wildfire burning up the joy in the hearts of my children for years, started by a match lit early in my youth that slowly burned up the lives of those I was supposed to love with the fire of my neglect. So now, under these very charged conditions, I have elected willfully to come forward, unlike so many of the cowardice absent fathers before me, to explain in the best way I can the reasons for our negligence and our continued absence in the lives of the children we have given life to. It would be ignorant for me not to acknowledge that for most of you still bleeding from the wounds that we as deadbeat dads have inflicted upon the innocence of your person, you would openly accept our reasons for not being present for all these years as a justifiable excuse given to wipe away all the tears you cried as a result of the pain you were forced to endure because of our failures. I know you are not going to take kindly to me asking you for anything, but if you would just this once try your best to process the words you are about to hear from my mouth objectively, then just maybe, by the time I come to the end of my answer to the whys of your question I can at least provide you with some of the answers you would need to successfully move on in your life journey, if you choose to, either with or without me. Now that I have at least attempted to lay a sturdy enough foundation to begin framing my answer to stand up long enough for you all to process the credibility of its strength while it continues to sink down into the quick-sands of the inexcusable, I will first begin, with what I believe is extremely significant for your understanding of my explanation, to explain at this moment, *What I See When I Look at You Looking at the Failure in Me!*

I am not blind to the reality of how it is you all see me. In your silence, your pain speaks loudly through the chapters of your life story with pages inked in the unhealed bloody scars left from the knife I stabbed you in the heart with. The vicious looks that boil with the fury of your disgrace, I assume conveyed your mali-cious intentions when you mean mugged me, sug-gesting you were shamed by my existence and even more offended by the show of my presence after be-ing absent for so long. Your failed attempts not to even acknowledge my existence when I waltzed in and out of your staged reality as significant to the person you have become epitomizes in you a reflection of me, the behavior of the man you hate, a hatred that caused you to become me, the man you did not want to be. I am here today because when I look at you, you re-mind me of a beauty that once possessed the innocence of my soul before I began to mingle around aimless-ly with a host of demonic forces personally designed for me, and those forces unconfronted because of the

continued failures of my father's contentment with residing in the ignorance bundled all up in a generation
of curses. Because of the insecurities I never managed
to confront within myself, I resented you because the
beauty of your innocence never allowed me to use my
failure as a justified excuse to disqualify myself from a
fatherly office that came without instructions outlining
the details of its responsibility. I ran from you because
you reminded me of the potential possibility of what I
could have become, the individual I willingly forfeited being because of my addictive obsession and selfish
delight with my exotic sin.

My failure to readily employ for your availability
the services and resources assigned to me because of
the consequences of my office reflects the arrogant ignorance of my prideful posture concerned only with
the enabling applause of strangers celebrating me for
the success of accolades unachieved at the costly expense of jeopardizing the value of a relationship with
the heirs to the legacy of the family throne that would
forever acknowledge our contributions to the world
in the chronicles of our generational success. The repercussions of my action towards you were a tragedy
deeply merged into the historical fabric of our family pedigree. This tragedy is linked to generations of
fathers whose failure to confront the evil assigned to

sabotage their character paved the way for the demons of my father and my father's father to skip down through lines of generations and jump onto the shoulders of descendants obscured by the difficulty of their already burdensome destiny. Let me make this clear! Even though I am the one speaking in the courtroom today, the almost fatal wound of fatherlessness we see happening all around the world is not a weight that can be carried by me alone but rather a weight created by generations of fatherly conspirators that measured the integrity of their morality by using the instability of their own selfishness to justify the excuses for their negligence. Like fathers carrying the demons of their fathers and their father's father on their shoulders, you, the wounded, are carrying the generational wounds of the afflicted and, if not cured, you will go and continue to afflict punishment on the innocent of your own prodigy.

To experience true liberation, however, the mind of both the oppressed and the oppressor must be explored and successfully liberated for the two sides to reconcile. I was once oppressed, residing in a false sense of entitlement stemming from my pain, waiting to no end for my father to come and rescue me from the overwhelming feeling of unworthiness. Dismissing my pain, as if my refusal to acknowledge its existence would eliminate its influence upon my impression, deceived me into believing I was totally cured from the need for my father's presence, only to come to find out that I became the replacement for the failure of his existence after his death. Once the oppressed but now the oppressor, I am sitting here in a room filled with the rage of the angry and disgruntled, trying to explain how to heal when both the offended and the offender live within the same space called me. It is hard to return the offending offense back into the hands of its rightful owner when the offended and the offender reside in the same space called you.

I say all that to say, before coming here today to face the fear of your wrath from which I have been running away from for years, I had to acknowledge the pain I inflicted upon you, accept full responsibility for poisoning the wounds you tried to bandage up, but that still bleed and forgive myself for the things I am embarrassed about before coming to the stand. I cannot make it up to you for all the wrong I have done, and if you choose either to do or not to do life with me after this, I still have to have some peace to live out the rest of my life comfortably for myself. The only way any of us can ever undo the wrongs we have done to the people we were supposed to love is by embracing the challenge of learning how to love the enemy in us the right way so that we can love the heirs of our legacy the way God always knew they needed to be loved, for them to conqueror over those forces attempting to silence the stories of their success. At the time, your mother and I divorced the shamefulness of a marriage, once lit by what we presumed was an eternal flame that ended up burning out, seemingly overpowered because of our unpreparedness for the scorching wildfires that terrorize our harvest in the seeds sown within the land of our promise, impaired my judgment with anger that charged your mother with the crimes of my mistakes.

I understand now that the grace I am asking you for is not the same grace I extended towards you during the early hours of my resentment.

I loved your mother and honestly entered into our union expecting us to always and forever be. Somewhere along the way, however, when the unbearable loneliness I experienced at times in our companionship became more frustrating than the loneliness I experienced in isolation, I ran to flee from the presence of all the things and people that constantly reminded me of the unfulfilled pleasures that helped to empty out all the water from my springing well of happiness. I was unhappy with myself, with my marriage, and with life in general. I did not have any more patience or the know-how to disregard my feelings to hope for a change in my situation so that the outcome could have benefited you all more than myself.

I tried to rid myself of the pain of my mistakes by placing the heaviness of all the blame for the failures that occurred within my life experience on your mother and the under-developed shoulders of your youthful innocence. I expected you to be mature enough to somehow bear up under the weight of a burden you were not mature enough to handle the responsibility of. To my sons, I expected you to act like a man without ever effectively modeling for you the behaviors of how a real man acts and what a real man looks like. To my daughters, I never modeled for you the highest standard of manhood that would have allowed you to set a realistic bar to measure up the attitude of approach coming from the men pursuing after the value of your potential as they attempted in their childish efforts to walk beside you as the King God elected to cover with honor the grace of your Queen. You have instead been prematurely exposed to the shameful realities of life through trials and errors that have hindered your ability to process the possibility of your potential to be the perfected form of the original God destined for you to become!

I am so sorry for not affirming for you that voice inside calling you to the higher dimensions of greatness to which you, because of me, were under-prepared to go! It was the voice of God calling you to play the role He scripted for you to play in a story He authored. I was supposed to be the primary source of understanding for you, but my absence caused you to err in your ignorance, altered by an entitlement that caused you to believe you had a right to do whatever you felt until you received the true answer to the reasons for your WHY. *Why did I choose not to father you after things ended between your mother and me? Why did I not claim you as my son, my daughter? Why did I not model for you the evolution of a maleness committed to the responsibility of manhood? Why did I never reach for you when you needed me? Why did I not protect you from the pain of my failures? Why did I not show you the posture and attitude with which a real Godly man should approach the pressures of real-life issues? Why, why, no, how could I forget to preserve the legacy of my name for you, my son, my daughter? Why did I never make you fill like you were enough?*

Please understand that what I am about to say is in no way intended to be condescending, but the answer to these questions is hard and impossible for me to explain for you to understand through the powerlessness of my words. Any answer I choose to provide you with at this point, within the obvious dysfunction of our relations, will not provide you with the answers you have desired to hear. The 'Why' will not stop the bleeding but possibly make it worse off for all of us. But even though that may be true, you still deserve an answer. The reason *why I choose not to father you after things ended between your mother and me. The reason for why I did not claim you as my son. The reason why I did not model for you the evolution of a maleness committed to the responsibility of true manhood. The reason why I never reached for you when you needed me. The reason why I never protected you from the pain of my failures? The reason why I never showed you the posture or attitude with which a real Godly man should approach the pressures of real-life issues? The reason why, no, how could I have forgotten to preserve the legacy of my name for you, my son, my daughter, my child? The reason why I never managed to make you fill like you were ever enough.*

The reason for my 'Why' to all these questions that have harassed you for years is because I, as your father, have always known you needed me, but I was selfishly unwilling to provide you with my provision because I cared more about myself than I cared about you. Speaking honestly, you were the line of memories I excitedly snorted away to erase the image of your existence from my imagination. The overwhelming sensational attraction with my selfish ambition in relation to the echoing sound of your roaring request of me at

the time never seemed to measure equally in the bal-
ance of my priorities. I did not consider you my prior-
ity but a menace to a problematic cancer I needed to
erase out of the history of a story I wrote but no longer
wanted to remember. You were the stain I needed to
wipe away from my past for me to embrace the cele-
bratory applause of strangers that touted the success
of my conducted character from a concocted bio laced
with a host of accolades that made me look good on
paper. The wrath of my fury only continued to intensify after my ex-wife, your mother, forced me to comply
with financially supporting your legitimacy as ordered
to do so by a judge. I only remembered you because, at
the end of every month, you choked the hell out of my
monthly income, burdening me with the overwhelming responsibility for your financial care and concern.
This is the true answer to all the questions you waited
for me all these years to resolve with the reasons for
my why.

As hard as it is for me to admit, this is the shameful
image of the father I was, but not the last impression
of the kind of father I want you to remember me to be.
The ignorant absence of the father I was supposed to
be was riddled with the bullet holes of self-inflected
wounds, shot through a cannon fully loaded with cus-
tom-made ammunition thrust through the generational

channels of my fatherly pedigree that savagely tampered an atmosphere of success with the residue of gun powder and projectiles that led child detectives all way back to the origin of the curse. There are no excuses for my actions, and today I take full responsibility and announce that I alone was the leader of my own choices. Even though there are many other factors you may have not taken into consideration regarding the influences behind my decision, I will not stand on the shoulders of that logic to justify my wrong because I, like you, had a choice. If there is one thing in the world that God does not control, it is the human will. Our human will, without acknowledging God's existence, prioritizes the value of the objectives and individuals it encounters through the darkness of blind eyes rather than with God's eyes that postures us all with an appreciation for the authenticity of their Godly worth. My stubbornness blinded me, not allowing me to see you in the capacity God naturally created you to exist in. I expected you, without my guiding affirmation, to be unaffected by my absence on your journey to success. Even though I was born looking like my parents, I know now that I will die looking like my decisions. My choice not to be there for you has caused me to experience the pains of my death slowly, all while my hopes and aspiration seem to dissolve quickly. Remember this, you can choose to do in this life whatever you want to do, but you cannot choose the consequences or the outcome of where your decisions will take you after this life is over.

I chose the pleasure of my sin over you, and that is a mistake I wish I could, but I know I will never be able to take back. Yes, to some degree, my thinking about you has changed because of the difficulties of my experience and all the times I rehearsed in my mind how things may have been different between us if only you would have seen my footsteps in the sand. If I would have carried you, you would have never had to walk alone in the valley of the unknown to mingle around in isolation with trial and error. I should have been there to protect you and show you how to protect yourself from the enemies you could see and the ones you could not see. I was not there, but I AM HERE NOW BECAUSE I CHOSE YOU!

Although I cannot make up for all the hurt I have caused you, I choose from this point forward to rest in your presence, burdened down by the shame of my mistakes, to fight for your love and respect because, without you, my time in this life will be unfulfilled. I decided years ago to do today what I should have done long ago, choose you first. You are my children, and even when in my ignorance I tried to forget about you, I could never get you out of my mind. As strange as it may sound, I am telling you the truth, but I struggled with the notion that I was worthy enough to make up for, with the time I have left, the sour taste of my fatherly neglect, with better memories to replace the absence of my image when you are moved to observe the details of your pain. You may be asking where was this urgency with which I now am pursuing after you when you longed for me to be the fatherly defender of your innocence. Back then, I was blinded by the unfulfilling promises of my fantasied reality, by which I thrust all my energy into pursuing after, only to discover that true fulfillment resides in the peace bound up in the heart of the children touched by the love of their father. I have been unfulfilled for years, disguising my own wounds with an unrealistic façade featuring the catastrophe of my failure through the weaknesses that ultimately revealed to the world your strength. Though wounded, you keep fighting, learning how to do the opposite from the lessons of my mistakes, how to cultivate the ground for the seeds you planted to ensure the health and prosperity of your harvest.

Yes, despite the lack of my efforts toward you, you have done well thus far. For the kind of fight you are fighting, however, well is not enough. As I said before, to win over the demonic forces that have sabotaged the highest-ranking human office on earth, fatherhood, you and I are going to have to work together. We, right now at this moment, can establish ourselves as the pioneers that called for a cease-fire between us, laying a traceable foundation for the hearts of the fathers to turn back towards their children and the hearts of the children back toward their fathers. The victory of our defeat is celebrated in the casualties of our dividedness. If we continue to fight in isolation, we cannot defeat the evil forces that broadcast the normalcy of fatherlessness in a world dedicated to expelling the irreplaceable role of the father from the core of the family structure. It does not matter if you like me because, honestly, I still struggle with liking myself for all the wrong I have done to you. I totally understand your dislike and lack of love for me. You do not trust me, nor should you. When I first carried you, I dropped you because my mind was not strong enough to bear up under the burden of your weight. The call to which God laid upon you to reveal the excellence of His greatness to the world intimidated me into conforming to the lust of my weakness, justifying my reasons for not having to embrace the load of your weight I assumed I was unable to carry. I came to discover, however, that dead weight is much heavier to carry than a life secured in the abundantly fulfilling weight of destiny.

The cost of abandonment is a much heavier price to pay than the much lighter weight of embracing the responsibility of nurturing you. Believe it or not, your absence in my life challenged me every day to confront the enemy in me that I was running away from! Now I am stronger! I am wiser! I am better, so much better! I am here now to avenge your innocence and to build a bond with you that will make it possible for us to restore the confidence in the hearts of your children and your children's children to trust again in the safety of a bridge called fatherhood.

My strength failed me before because I tried carrying the weight of God's glory on you without joy in the Lord which is where I needed to obtain my strength to carry you in the beginning. I will never attempt to love you the way I know you need to be loved again in my own strength, but now I know I can do all things through Christ who strengthens me to do what I cannot do on my own. The wrong I have done, I cannot change! What I can change, however, is the good energy with which I pursue after your heart from this point forward. I am chasing after you, and I will continue to chase after you until your heart turns to greet me with arms open wide. If you never turn, I will continue to chase after you! If you continue to question the sincerity of my plea to you, I will chase after you more aggressively until my actions cause you to question the logic that influences the attitude of your conviction. You asked me why and I believe I have answered. So, what are you going to do now that you have the answers to the questions you have been longing to hear? At the beginning of this discourse, you passed the ball to me to see if I would take the last shot. I am quite sure you never thought I would pass it back to you. The ball is in your court now, and what you do on the court under the lights at this moment will cause your children to compare your legacy to greats like Kobe and Michael or to the weakness of 76ers star Ben Simmons, who was afraid to shoot the ball. The legacy you leave now is up to you. The masterpiece of greatness is never revealed in the moments of your contributions but rather in the revolving integrity of those individuals granted the opportunity to be great once they realize you trust them to shoot the game-winning shot. Regardless of whether or not they hit the game-winning shot, as the superstar veteran of the team, instilling the confidence in the members of your team that you will continue to pass the ball to them until they make it maximizes their potential to achieve God's greatness in the context of time God has awarded them.

In the early years of my fatherly career, I played in isolation, with no regard for the players on my team. I

James Harden you! I shot my shots without ever thinking to pass the ball to you so that you might come to rediscover the presence of your greatness within you. It does not matter how many points in life I scored because without you on the court beside me, I can never win. I never raised my hands in the victories I attempted to achieve without you. I lost every time, and I have been losing ever since. I made the adjustments I wanted to make in order to employ my efforts to ensure the possibility of victory, but I still lost because I chose not to follow the instruction of my coach. But when I humbled myself and followed the advice of my head coach, G.O.D, then I began to understand that we were not only teammates, but more importantly, we were family. Like Kobe and Shaq, we have bumped heads, but now we must rebuild the collapsed bridges we will have to walk across to unite us by nullifying our generational dividedness while observing the scenery on the generational caravan of love.

So, what are you going to do with the weapons you have in your hands? Are you going to kill me, or are you going to love me? Will you hate me for the rest of your life, or are you going to forgive me? Are you done with me, or will you give me another chance to make us right again? The ball is in your court! Either shoot your shot or pass the ball to your kids desiring for you to affirm their greatness. They are waiting for you. Be for them the superstar I failed to be for you. The strength of your leadership is not just up to you; it is up to us! THE SUCCESS OF THE FATHER CAN ONLY BE REVEALED THROUGH THE STRENGTH OF THE SON!

Notes

Chapter One

Quote on page 9 was taken from David Blankenhorn, *Fatherless America: Confronting Our Most Urgent Social Problems*, New York: Basic Books, 1995), 2.

Statistical reference on page 25 was taken from Myles Munroe, *The Fatherhood Principle* (New Kensington, PA: Whitaker House, 2008).

Quote on page 30 was taken from John Darby, *Ezekiel 18 Bible Commentary - John Darby's Synopsis - Christianity.* https://www.christianity.com/bible/commentary/ john-darby/ezekiel/18

Chapter Two

Quote on page 46 was taken from Mackenzie's poetry - *Blogger. https://theoddlifeofmackenzies.blogspot.com/*

Quote on page 47 was taken from Newsweek article: *Man Claiming to Be Bill Clinton's Son Wants Second DNA Test - Newsweek. https://www.newsweek.com/man-claiming-bill-clintons-son-wants-another-dna-test-980618*

Chapter 3

Quote on page 53 was taken from Shaun Saunders, 2 *Love Her No More!: The Superhero Lover's Saga Continues*, Atlanta: Shaun Saunders, 2019), 13.

Other Books by the Author

The Wounded Leader
(ISBN 978-0-615-65497-3)

The Superhero's Tell All Exclusive Interview
(ISBN 978-0-692-02244-3)

The Superhero Lover
(ISBN 978-0-692-77960-6)

Addiction
(ISBN 978-0-578-93457-0)

2 Love Her No More
(ISBN 978-0-578-47952-1)

Available from the author, in retail stores, on www.amazon.com, www.barnesandnoble. com, and wherever books are sold.

Contact Information

To inquire about Shaun Saunders speaking, ministering, or doing book signings and discussions at your event, you may contact him by sending an email to:

ssaunders89@yahoo.com

www.ingramcontent.com/pod-product-compliance
Lightning Source LLC
Chambersburg PA
CBHW052101150726
48002CB00002B/982